CRYSTAR™
CRYSTAL WARRIOR™

The Origin Of Crystar

by
David Anthony Kraft
Alan Kupperberg
and
Marie Severin

MARVEL® BOOKS

CRYSTAR™ THE CRYSTAL WARRIOR (including all prominent characters featured
in this storybook), and the distinctive likenesses thereof, are trademarks of the Marvel
Comics Group.

Published by Marvel Books, a division of Cadence Industries Corporation, 387 Park
Avenue South, New York, NY 10016. Printed in Canada. ISBN: 0-939766-56-6

In a Universe far away there is a world filled with heroes and villains, dragons and wizards, crystal palaces and molten pits of magma.

It is a world of magic, a world ruled by two brothers, Crystar and Moltar.

This is the city of Galax on the world—Crystalium!

Once peace ruled the planet, but now Galax is battered by war between the forces of good and evil, Order and Chaos.

It is a battle that threatens to pit brother against brother.

One bright, sunny day, a strange visitor came to Galax. He went to the two brothers who ruled the city.

"Crystar and Moltar," said the visitor, "I have good news for you both!"

"I am Zardeth!" the visitor said. "I know your kingdom suffers greatly in the war with Chaos. I can save your city and give you great power and victory.

"But there is a price," said Zardeth. "You must promise to serve me!"

Crystar did not like the wizard. "I think Zardeth is trying to trick us!" he thought.

"We of Galax are on Order's side!" said Crystar to Zardeth. "How do we know you are not an evil wizard of Chaos?"

But Moltar kept quiet. He liked what Zardeth said.

"The people of Galax are tired of war," thought Moltar. "Who cares if Chaos or Order rules?"

"Think about my offer!" Zardeth said, as he left. "Tell me your answer tomorrow at the Fountain of Fire."

"Crystar will not be fooled," thought Zardeth. "But I saw that Moltar was tricked by my words. Hah! Once I get those brothers to fight each other, Chaos will win!"

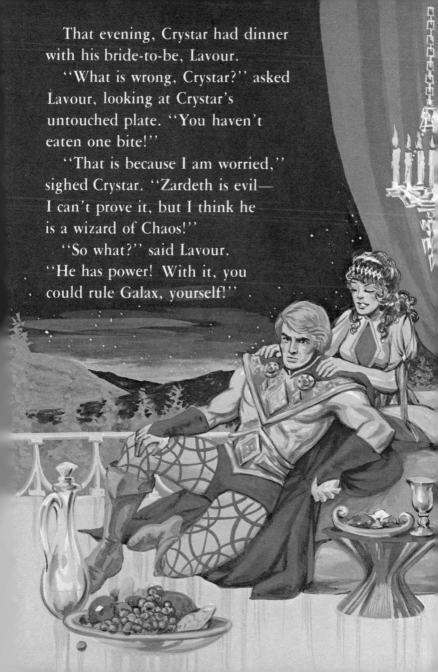

That evening, Crystar had dinner with his bride-to-be, Lavour.

"What is wrong, Crystar?" asked Lavour, looking at Crystar's untouched plate. "You haven't eaten one bite!"

"That is because I am worried," sighed Crystar. "Zardeth is evil— I can't prove it, but I think he is a wizard of Chaos!"

"So what?" said Lavour. "He has power! With it, you could rule Galax, yourself!"

The next day, the brothers met.

"I think we should take Zardeth's offer!" said Moltar. "The war would stop!"

"But what is the real price?" asked Crystar. "I cannot let our people become slaves of evil—of Chaos!"

"Bah!" shouted Moltar. "You are weak, Crystar. Only a weak man would have such fears! I am strong! That is why I should be Galax's only king!"

Just then, their uncle, Feldspar, entered.

"Why can't you two brothers work together?" asked Feldspar.

"Be quiet," shouted Moltar, pushing Feldspar, who tripped and fell. He was knocked out.

"Moltar—why did you do that?" said Crystar, stunned. "Feldspar was only trying to help us!"

"Shut up, Crystar!" said Moltar, striking down his brother in anger.

"Now there is only one king of Galax!" said Moltar. "I will tell the people of Zardeth's plan. They will be happy to follow me!"

Quickly, Moltar told the people of Galax about Zardeth's offer of peace and power.

Lavour was the first to join Moltar. She wanted power as much as Moltar did.

Many men and women, tired of all the fighting, happily lined up behind Moltar and Lavour. They would join Zardeth.

Meanwhile, Ambara, Lavour's serving girl, discovered the fallen Crystar and Feldspar. "I must help them," she thought.

"But what can I do? They are too heavy for me to move!"

Just then, Ambara heard a strange noise.

Suddenly, a big ball of bright light entered the room. Fearing evil magic, Ambara tried to shield Crystar.

But the light grew bigger and brighter. Soon, it filled the whole room. Then, Ambara heard the sound of a powerful wind.

"The light is taking us away!" said Ambara. "But where are we going?"

Ambara found herself in a strange room.

"I am Ogeode," said a mysterious figure. "In the early days, it was I who drove the forces of Chaos from this world. Now, I must act again!"

Suddenly, the light and wind stopped. Ambara looked around — she was in a wizard's room!

"Magic cannot save your kingdom, brave Crystar," said Ogeode. "Only your own courage can."

Weakly, Crystar asked, "How?"

Ogeode said, "You must walk into the mystic Prisma-Crystal. When you come out, you will be *more* than a normal man. You will be a crystal warrior!"

"The risk is great!" said Ogeode, as Crystar stood up. "But it is the only way the forces of Order can beat Zardeth and Chaos!"

"Then, what you say shall be done!" said Crystar. "I will enter the Prisma-Crystal!"

Crystar walked into the gem. An hour passed, but nothing seemed to happen.

"We have tried, but we have failed," sighed Ogeode. "I shall heal Feldspar and we must carry on. But I fear the forces of Chaos have gained an upper hand this day!"

"No, we must have hope!" said Ambara. "Somehow, we will win!"

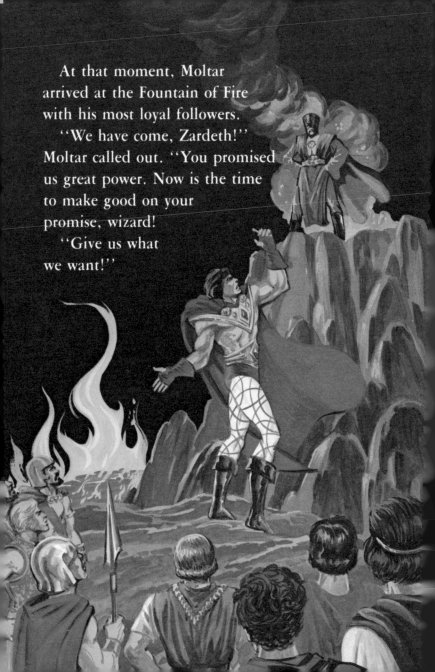

At that moment, Moltar arrived at the Fountain of Fire with his most loyal followers.

"We have come, Zardeth!" Moltar called out. "You promised us great power. Now is the time to make good on your promise, wizard!

"Give us what we want!"

"You shall have power, my greedy friend."
Zardeth replied. "Behold the fury of the
planet, herself!

"It is in this burning pit of Magma that you
shall get power to rule all of Crystalium! And it
is in this pit that you will become willing slaves
of Chaos!"

When Moltar and his people came out of the steaming lava pit, they were no longer normal men—they were terrible Magma Men!

"Behold! You have great power—and immortality! You are invincible! You will feel no pain! You are all ten times stronger than any human! You are Magma Men! This is how you shall serve Chaos!" shouted Zardeth.

Meanwhile, back at the palace of Ogeode, a bright light suddenly filled the great chamber! Ambara and Ogeode stepped back in surprise and shock!

"What is happening?" asked Ambara.

"I don't dare guess!" said Ogeode. "Could it be..."

"...it is!" shouted Ogeode. "It's CRYSTAR—THE CRYSTAL WARRIOR!"

"I have faced the challenge of the great Prisma-Crystal," said Crystar, his voice ringing out like a bell. "Its great magic changed me into a champion for Order!"

"There is no time to lose!" said Ogeode. "We must act now!"

"Our people will no longer stand helpless before the evil of Moltar and Zardeth!" said Ambara.

"Yes," agreed Feldspar, who had been healed by Ogeode. "But remember, Crystar—Moltar is your brother. Seek peace, not revenge!"

"I will remember," said Crystar. "But first, Zardeth and Chaos must be stopped!"

Outside the city of Galax, Moltar led his Magma Men in an attack. Their mission was to storm Ogeode's palace and steal the precious Prisma-Crystal.

The normal people of Galax were no match for Moltar's Magma Men.

The people of Galax were afraid.

In the royal palace, the captains called Stalax, Warbow and Koth were startled when the changed Crystar strode into the room.

"Crystar!" Koth shouted. "What has happened to you?"

"You must help us!" said Stalax. "Moltar and his Magma Men are attacking Galax!"

Crystar turned to Ogeode and said, "It is true that I have great power. But I am only one man. Moltar has an army."

"I can make you all strong enough to stop Moltar and his men!" said Ogeode. "By focusing my magic through Crystar, I can make you crystal warriors—just like Crystar!"

"Crystal warriors must have weapons of crystal!" said Ogeode.

"Not even Zardeth can make better weapons!"

Just when it looked like Moltar and his evil Magma Men had won, Crystar and his great crystal warriors attacked!

"Where did you get your power?" shouted the surprised Moltar.

"From Order!" said Crystar. "And my army will not stop fighting until we have won peace on Crystalium!"

Soon, Moltar was running away with his beaten army.

Then, Crystar saw a strange man step out from behind a rock. It was a man who was half magma and half crystal. Suddenly, Crystar saw that the man was his uncle, Feldspar!

"Feldspar, what happened to you?" asked Crystar.

"I am a man of peace. I want peace between you and your brother. I have become a symbol of that peace," said Feldspar.

"So long as Moltar serves the cause of Chaos, I must fight him," said Crystar. "But let your sacrifice be the symbol of the great hope of Order—